OBELIX AND CO.

TEXT BY GOSCINNY
DRAWINGS BY UDERZO

TRANSLATED BY ANTHEA BELL AND DEREK HOCKRIDGE

HODDER DARGAUD
LONDON SYDNEY AUCKLAND

ASTERIX IN OTHER COUNTRIES

Australia	Hodder Dargaud, Mill Road, Dunton Green, Sevenoaks, Kent TN13 2XX, England
Austria	Delta Verlag, Postfach 1215, 7 Stuttgart 1, G.F.R.
Belgium	Dargaud Bénélux, 3 rue Kindermans, 1050 Brussels
Brazil	Cedibra, rua Filomena Nunes 162, Rio de Janeiro
Canada	Dargaud Canada, 307 Benjamin-Hudon, St. Laurent, Montreal P.Q. H4N1J1
Denmark	Gutenberghus Bladene, Vognmagergade 11, 1148 Copenhagen K
Finland	Sanoma Osakeyhtio, Ludviginkatu 2–10, 00130 Helsinki 13
France	Dargaud Editeur, 12 rue Blaise-Pascal, P.O. Box 155, 92201 Neuilly Sur Seine
	(Breton) Armor Diffusion, 59 rue Duhamel, 35100 Rennes
	(Langue d'Oc) Société Toulousaine du Livre, Avenue de Larrieu, 31094 Toulouse
German Federal Republic	Delta Verlag, Postfach 1215, 7 Stuttgart 1, G.F.R.
Greece	Anglo-Hellenic Agency, Kriezotou 3, Syntagma, Athens 134, Greece
Holland	Dargaud Bénélux, 3 rue Kindermans, 1050 Brussels, Belgium
	(Distribution) Oberon, Ceylonpoort 5–25, Haarlem, Holland
Hong Kong	Hodder Dargaud, Mill Road, Dunton Green, Sevenoaks, Kent TN13 2XX, England
Iceland	Fjolvi HF, Njorvasund 15a, Reykjavik
Indonesia	Pt Sinar Kasih, Tromolpos 260, Jakarta
Italy	Arnoldo Mondadori Editore, 1 Via Belvedere, 37131 Verona
Latin America	Grijalbo-Dargaud S.A., Deu y Mata 98, Barcelona 14
New Zealand	Hodder Dargaud, Mill Road, Dunton Green, Sevenoaks, Kent TN13 2XX, England
Norway	A/S Hjemmet (Gutenburghus Group), Kristian den 4des Gate 13, Oslo 1
Portugal	Meriberica, rua D. Filipa de Vilherna 4–5°, Lisbon
Roman Empire	*(Latin)* Delta Verlag, Postfach 1215, 7 Stuttgart 1, G.F.R.
South Africa	*(English)* Hodder Dargaud, Mill Road, Dunton Green, Sevenoaks, Kent TN13 2XX, England
Spain	Grijalbo-Dargaud S.A., Deu y Mata 98, Barcelona 14
Sweden	Hemmets Journal Forlag (Gutenburghes Group), Fack, 200 22 Malmo
Switzerland	Interpress Dargaud S.A., En Budron B, 1052 Le Mont/Lausanne
Turkey	Kervan Kitabcilik, Serefendi Sokagi 31, Cagaloglu-Istanbul
Wales	*(Welsh)* Gwasg Y Dref Wen, 28 Church Road, Yr Eglwys Newydd, Cardiff CF4 2EA
Yugoslavia	Nip Forum, Vojvode Misica 1–3, 2100 Novi Sad

British Library Cataloguing in Publication Data
Goscinny
 Obelix and Co
 I. Title. II. Bell, Anthea III. Hockridge, Derek
 IV. Uderzo
 741'5.944   PN6747 G6

ISBN 0 340 22709 5 (cased edition)
ISBN 0 340 25307 X (paperbound edition)

First published in Great Britain 1978 (cased)
Second impression 1979

First published in Great Britain 1980 (paperbound)

Printed in Belgium for Hodder Dargaud Ltd,
Mill Road, Dunton Green, Sevenoaks, Kent TN13 2YJ
(Editorial Office: 47 Bedford Square, London WC1B 3DP)
by Henri Proost & Cie, Turnhout

GAULISH VILLAGE

COMPENDIUM

LAUDANUM

AQUARIUM

TOTORUM

ARMORICA

BELGICA

LUTETIA

SPQR

GAUL
(ROMAN CONQUEST)
50 B.C.

CELTICA

AQUITANIA

PROVINCIA

The year is 50 BC. Gaul is entirely occupied by the Romans.
Well, not entirely… One small village of indomitable Gauls still
holds out against the invaders. And life is not easy for the
Roman legionaries who garrison the fortified camps of
Totorum, Aquarium, Laudanum and Compendium…

a few of the Gauls

Asterix, the hero of these adventures. A shrewd, cunning little warrior; all perilous missions are immediately entrusted to him. Asterix gets his superhuman strength from the magic potion brewed by the druid Getafix...

Obelix, Asterix's inseparable friend. A menhir delivery-man by trade; addicted to wild boar. Obelix is always ready to drop everything and go off on a new adventure with Asterix — so long as there's wild boar to eat, and plenty of fighting.

Getafix, the venerable village druid. Gathers mistletoe and brews magic potions. His speciality is the potion which gives the drinker superhuman strength. But Getafix also has other recipes up his sleeve...

Cacofonix, the bard. Opinion is divided as to his musical gifts. Cacofonix thinks he's a genius. Everyone else thinks he's unspeakable. But so long as he doesn't speak, let alone sing, everybody likes him...

Finally, Vitalstatistix, the chief of the tribe. Majestic, brave and hot-tempered, the old warrior is respected by his men and feared by his enemies. Vitalstatistix himself has only one fear; he is afraid the sky may fall on his head tomorrow. But as he always says, 'Tomorrow never comes.'

DISCIPLINE IS FAIRLY LAX IN THE FORTIFIED ROMAN CAMP OF TOTORUM...

IT'S OUR RELIEF, BOYS! IT'S OUR RELIEF!

OPEN THE GATES! OPEN THE GATES!

HEY, CENTURION SCROFULUS! IT'S THEM ALL RIGHT!

I AM CENTURION IGNORAMUS! AVE!

HI! I'M CENTURION SCROFULUS... AVE! WHAT A RELIEF!

NOT IN UNIFORM, CENTURION SCROFULUS?

WE HARDLY EVER GO OUT, SO WE DON'T BOTHER TO DRESS UP.

SCRATCH! SCRATCH!

FORWARD MARCH!

I LIKE A NICE MARCH PAST, I DO!

EH?

A WORD OF ADVICE... TAKE IT EASY AND WAIT FOR YOUR RELIEF. AND IGNORE ANY PROVOCATION FROM THE LOCAL GAULS. THEY'RE CRAZY. THEY'RE ALSO INVINCIBLE.

I HAVE EVERY INTENTION OF BRINGING THOSE VERY GAULS TO HEEL! THAT WILL PLEASE JULIUS CAESAR... AND I DON'T WANT TO STAY A CENTURION MY WHOLE LIFE LONG!

SOUNDS LIKE YOUR WHOLE LIFE WON'T BE LONG... WELL, GET MOVING, LADS!

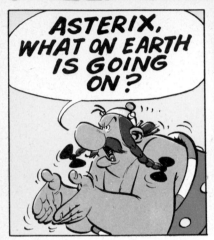

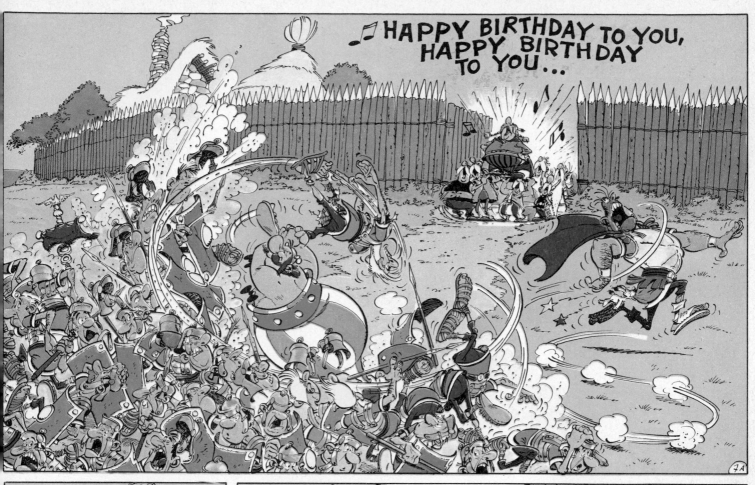

IN ROME...

ONE MAN! ONE SOLITARY GAUL MANAGED TO DEFEAT AND DEMORALISE MY CRACK TROOPS!

THIS IS TOO MUCH! THESE GAULS MAKE ME LOOK RIDICULOUS. WE CAN'T GO ON LIKE THIS, BY JUPITER! WELL? I'M WAITING FOR SUGGESTIONS!

WE COULD SEND THE ENTIRE ARMY...

YES, BUT WE MUSTN'T LEAVE OUR FRONTIERS UNGUARDED.

SUPPOSE WE SET UP A COMMISSION TO STUDY THE PROBLEM?

GOOD IDEA! WITH SUB-COMMITTEES TO CONSIDER THE VARIOUS ASPECTS...

LET'S HAVE A WORKING LUNCH TO DISCUSS IT...

TAPTAPTAP! TAPTAP!

THEY ARE STRONG, SO WE MUST WEAKEN THEM. THEY HAVE NOTHING TO DO BUT FIGHT, SO WE MUST KEEP THEM BUSY SOME OTHER WAY...

COME HERE, CAIUS PREPOSTERUS. JUST HOW WOULD YOU SET ABOUT WEAKENING THE GAULS, WITH THEIR MAGICAL STRENGTH?

GO ON! LET'S SEE WHAT THEY TAUGHT YOU AT THE LATIN SCHOOL OF ECONOMICS...

EASY, O CAESAR. GOLD, THE PROFIT MOTIVE...

...WILL ENFEEBLE THEM AND KEEP THEM BUSY. WE MUST CORRUPT THEM.

YOU THINK THAT WILL DO THE TRICK?

LOOK AROUND YOU, O CAESAR!

NONSENSE!

THAT YOUNG KNOW-ALL HAS NO EXPERIENCE!

DON'T LISTEN TO HIM, O CAESAR. WHAT WE NEED IS A THINK TANK...

WE MUST OPPOSE FORCE WITH FORCE! REMEMBER OUR CAMPAIGNS, CAESAR? WE MADE THE WHOLE WORLD BOW BEFORE OUR LEGIONS!

I REMEMBER ALL RIGHT, LARCENUS. YOU WERE A BRAVE, ATHLETIC YOUNG TRIBUNE, YOU BROUGHT BACK A FORTUNE FROM OUR CAMPAIGNS... AND NOW LOOK AT YOU!

SEE WHAT ALL YOUR GOLD, YOUR VILLAS, YOUR ORGIES HAVE MADE OF YOU! YOU'RE DECADENT!

YOU, A THINK TANK? ALL YOU THINK OF IS TANKING UP!

HMPH? LUNCHTIME?

~YOU REALLY THINK YOU CAN TURN THOSE CRAZY GAULS INTO SOMETHING LIKE THEM?

YES, CAESAR!

MARK MY WORDS, THEY'LL SOON HAVE TOO MUCH ON THEIR MINDS TO GO FIGHTING!

BUT I'LL NEED GOLD ... LOTS OF GOLD!

YOU SHALL HAVE UNLIMITED CREDIT! GET TO WORK PRE- POSTEROUS!

SEVERAL DAYS LATER, IN THE CAMP OF TOTORUM...

YES, HE'S A FAT MAN. OFTEN GOES FOR WALKS WITH A MENHIR ON HIS BACK AND A LITTLE DOG AT HIS HEELS...

YOU MIGHT WELL RUN INTO HIM IN THE FOREST... SO WATCH OUT! EVEN THE LITTLE DOG IS DANGEROUS.

I'M OFF. YOU MEN, DON'T LEAVE CAMP.

NOT LIKELY! WE'RE NOT LEAVING TILL WE'RE RELIEVED.

SOON AFTERWARDS...

PICKED UP A SCENT? LET'S HAVE A LOOK...

GRRRRRR!

?

OH, HOW BEAUTIFUL! JUST LOOK WHAT'S BEHIND YOU!

BEHIND ME?

BUT THERE ISN'T ANYTHING BEHIND ME!

YES, THERE IS! THAT MENHIR!

OH YES, I FORGOT... IT'S ONLY A MENHIR.

MAGNIFICENT!

?

14

WHERE DID YOU FIND IT?

I DIDN'T FIND IT, I MADE IT. I MAKE MENHIRS AND THEN I DELIVER THEM.

DO YOU DELIVER MANY?

NO, ONCE PEOPLE HAVE ONE MENHIR THEY DON'T WANT ANY MORE. MENHIRS DON'T WEAR OUT VERY FAST.

HOW MUCH IS IT?

OH, I DON'T KNOW ...I USUALLY SWAP THEM FOR SOMETHING

I'LL BUY IT! TWO HUNDRED SESTERTII!

SESTERTII?

YES! HAVING MONEY IS A GOOD THING. YOU CAN BUY ALL SORTS OF THINGS TO EAT... YOU'LL BE THE RICHEST MAN IN THE VILLAGE, AND THAT MEANS YOU'LL BE THE MOST INFLUENTIAL.

HERE YOU ARE.

IT'S A BIT HEAVY FOR ME... DELIVER IT TO THE CAMP OF TOTORUM.

THE CAMP OF TOTORUM?!?

NOOOOO! I'M NOT A LEGIONARY, I'M ONLY STAYING THERE! I'M A MENHIR BUYER... HERE, LET ME EXPLAIN.

GRRRAAOR!

A MENHIR BUYER AND A MENHIR DELIVERY MAN ARE JUST MADE TO DO BUSINESS...

LOOK AT THAT!

THE RELIEF?

NO! THE BIG FAT BRUTE!

15

NEXT DAY...

LOOK AT THAT!

THE RELIEF?

NO! THE BIG! FAT BRUTE!

TAKE COVER, ALL!

ISN'T THERE EVER ANYONE HERE?

WHAT A BEAUTY! IT'S EVEN BETTER THAN THE FIRST ONE!

HERE'S FOUR HUNDRED SESTERTII.

NO. TWO HUNDRED.

PRICES ARE GOING UP.

WHERE TO?

NO, NO... IT'S BECAUSE OF SUPPLY AND DEMAND... THE STATE OF THE MARKET... WELL, IT'S ALL RATHER COMPLICATED, BUT IT LEADS TO GALLOPING INFLATION.

AND DON'T FORGET, I'LL BUY ALL THE MENHIRS YOU CAN MAKE.

SNIFF! SNIFF!

ASTERIX!

YES?

I'M HUNGRY. DO YOU THINK...

WHEN YOU'RE NOT SO BUSY YOU CAN GO HUNTING BOAR AGAIN. THE FOREST'S FULL OF THEM.

SCRUNCH!

GRRRRR!

OH, HOW BEAUTIFUL, ANALGESIX! JUST LOOK WHAT'S BEHIND YOU!

?

IT'S ONLY A BOAR!

I KNOW IT'S A BOAR, YOU FOOL. LET ME HAVE IT!

ARE YOU CRAZY?

TAP! TAP! TAP!

HERE. YOU CAN USE THIS TO BUY THINGS, AND THEN YOU'LL BE THE SECOND RICHEST MAN IN THE VILLAGE.

AND I'LL BUY ALL YOU CAN DELIVER.

???

TOMORROW I'LL PAY YOU TWO HANDFULS OF COINS, BECAUSE PRICES ARE TROTTING THROUGH THE MARKET PLACE AND GETTING BLOWN UP IN THE AIR, AND IT'S ALL RATHER COMPLICATED.

!!!

DINNER TIME, ANALGESIX!

I CAN'T STOP! I'VE GOT WORK TO DO!

??

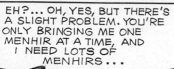

I DON'T THINK IT'S ANYTHING SERIOUS...

BUT WHAT BOTHERS ME IS THIS SUDDEN PASSION THE ROMANS HAVE FOR MENHIRS...

NOT BAD GOING, BUT I MUST TALK TO YOU... I SUGGEST WE HAVE A WORKING LUNCH.

THAT'S LUCKY. SOMETHING SEEMS TO HAVE KEPT MY HUNTERS IN THE FOREST TODAY.

PRODUCTION HAS INCREASED, BUT YOU STILL HAVE A DELIVERY PROBLEM. YOU NEED TO STEP UP THE EFFICIENCY OF YOUR DISTRIBUTION CHANNELS.

UH?

SORRY, I FORGOT... YOU NOT BRING PLENTY MENHIRS ALL ONE TIME. YOU BRING MORE MENHIRS QUICK QUICK!

ME NOT FIND PLENTY DELIVERY MEN...

WELL, THINK THE PROBLEM OVER. WE'LL BE IN TOUCH AND HAVE ANOTHER WORKING LUNCH.

AND ANOTHER THING: YOU WANT TO START SPENDING YOUR SESTERTII. YOU NEED SOME SMARTER CLOTHES...

WHY? WHAT'S THE MATTER WITH MY BREECHES?

IT'S NOT THE WAY FOR A MAN WHO'S DOING SO WELL IN MENHIRS TO DRESS.

IT ISN'T?

GERIATRIX, DARLING! WOOLIX THE PEDLAR IS HERE!

STOP ARGUING! THE PEDLAR'S HERE, AND JUST FOR ONCE YOU CAN DROP ME OFF ON THE SHIELD!

BUT PEDIMENTA DARLING, IT'S MY OFFICIAL SHIELD!

ROLL UP, ROLL UP! I'VE GOT SILK FROM LUGDUNUM,* VELVET FROM SAMAROBRIVA,* HOUR GLASSES FROM HELVETIA *...

THE WONDER OF WOOLIX

* LYONS
* AMIENS
* SWITZERLAND

THE VERY LATEST THING FROM LUTETIA... QUITE INEXPENSIVE.

CAN I, GERIATRIX DEAR?

YES, YES, MY LOVE!

WELL, WHAT DO YOU THINK?

YES, IT'S VERY SLIMMING.

CAN I PAY IN FISH?

ALL RIGHT. THIS ISN'T THE TIME AND PLAICE TO CARP!

I'LL BUY THE LOT!

?! ?! ?! ?! ?! ?! ?!

POM TIDDLEY POM!

SUPPER READY, MY LOVE?

NO, SUPPER IS NOT READY! GET IT YOURSELF. I'M BUSY!

BUSY DOING WHAT, MY PET?

OBELIX ASKED ME TO MAKE HIM SOME CLOTHES. HE'S GOING TO PAY HANDSOMELY...

I HAVEN'T A THING TO WEAR! AND SINCE I CAN'T COUNT ON YOU, I HAVE TO FIND SOME WAY TO EARN A BIT OF MONEY!

A LITTLE LATER...

NOW THAT FAT FOOL OBELIX IS MAKING A PILE WITH HIS MENHIRS MY WIFE'S BECOMING A REAL SEW-AND-SEW. I CAN'T GO ON LIKE THIS!

CALM DOWN! AFTER ALL, OBELIX IS MY FRIEND!

WELL, MY WIFE IS MAKING EYES AT YOUR FRIEND!

AND SHE'S NEVER LOOKED AT ANYONE BUT ME... IT'S INCREDIBLE!

YES, I'VE OFTEN THOUGHT SO MYSELF...

SO WHAT AM I TO DO?

NOTHING. I'LL TRY TO TALK TO OBELIX!

YOU JUST DO THAT, OR I SHALL MAKE YOUR FINE FRIEND EAT MY STICK!

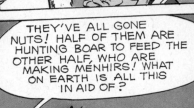

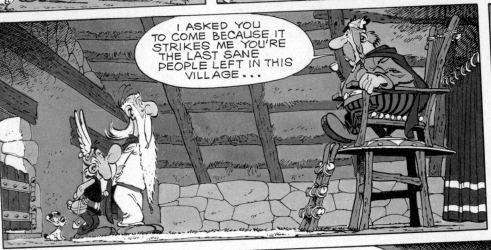

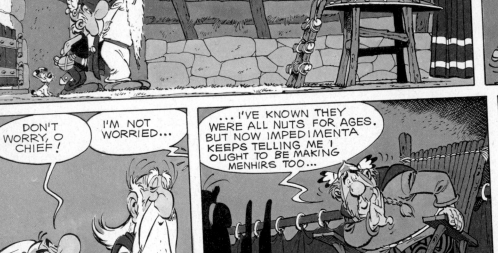

IN JULIUS CAESAR'S PALACE IN ROME...

AND JUST WHAT AM I SUPPOSED TO DO WITH ALL THESE MENHIRS?

BUT CAESAR, THOSE MENHIRS ARE THE PROOF OF MY SUCCESS! THE GAULS ARE TOO BUSY MAKING MENHIRS TO FIGHT, SO...

MAYBE, BUT YOU'RE DRAINING MY TREASURY TO KEEP A FEW MADMEN BUSY!

PEACE IS BEYOND ALL PRICE... SI VIS PACEM...

31A

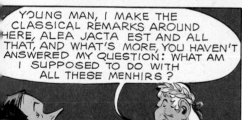

YOUNG MAN, I MAKE THE CLASSICAL REMARKS AROUND HERE, ALEA JACTA EST AND ALL THAT, AND WHAT'S MORE, YOU HAVEN'T ANSWERED MY QUESTION: WHAT AM I SUPPOSED TO DO WITH ALL THESE MENHIRS?

SELL THEM O CAESAR.

SELL THEM?

THAT'S RIGHT. THAT WAY, YOU NOT ONLY RECOVER YOUR EXPENSES, YOU MAKE A PROFIT TOO.

BUT WHO'D WANT MENHIRS? THEY'RE NO GOOD FOR ANYTHING!

PRECISELY! WE MUST DRAW UP A PLAN OF CAMPAIGN, DECIDE ON OUR STRATEGY, SET OUR SIGHTS ON THE RIGHT TARGET!

CAMPAIGN? STRATEGY? TARGET? THAT'S THE KIND OF THING I LIKE TO HEAR! I'LL GIVE ORDERS FOR THE LEGIONS TO PREPARE FOR BATTLE!

NO, NO! LET ME EXPLAIN...

31B

35

THE FOLLOWING PASSAGE WILL BE DIFFICULT FOR THOSE OF YOU UNACQUAINTED WITH THE ANCIENT BUSINESS WORLD TO UNDERSTAND, ESPECIALLY AS, THESE DAYS, SUCH A STATE OF AFFAIRS COULD NEVER EXIST, SINCE NO ONE WOULD DREAM OF TRYING TO SELL SOMETHING UTTERLY USELESS...

AT THIS PRESENT MOMENT IN TIME THE DEMAND FOR MENHIRS IS VIRTUALLY NIL. THEREFORE WE MUST BE CREATIVE... FIND HOW TO APPEAL TO THE POTENTIAL CONSUMER...

LET US STUDY THOSE FACTORS WHICH WILL ALLOW US TO HOME IN ON OUR TARGET...

PEOPLE WILL BUY: **A:** SOMETHING USEFUL; **B:** SOMETHING COMFORTABLE; **C:** SOMETHING THAT'S FUN; **D:** SOMETHING TO MAKE THE NEIGHBOURS ENVIOUS. WE HAVE TO AIM FOR **D**!

A CAMPAIGN CENTRED ON A CAREFULLY DEFINED AREA SHOULD ALLOW US TO MAKE RAPID CONTACT WITH A LARGE BODY OF CONSUMERS ABLE TO ABSORB OUR STOCKS AT MAXIMUM SPEED...

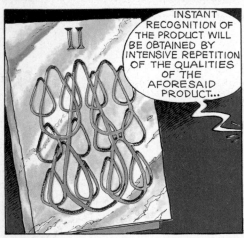

INSTANT RECOGNITION OF THE PRODUCT WILL BE OBTAINED BY INTENSIVE REPETITION OF THE QUALITIES OF THE AFORESAID PRODUCT...

...WHICH MAY BE DEFINED AS FOLLOWS: **A:** DURABILITY; **B:** SOLIDITY; **C:** OTHER QUALITIES.

THUS I MAKE NO RASH PROMISES WHEN I SAY THAT WE SHOULD SUCCEED IN OBTAINING POSITIVE RESULTS SALESWISE, AT NO VERY DISTANT DATE.

UH?

ME THINK YOU ABLE SELL HEAP BIG HEAP MENHIRS PLENTY QUICK.

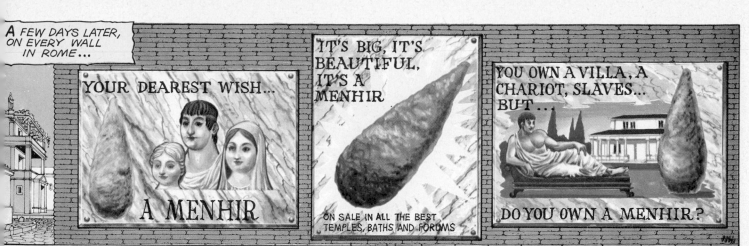

FREE GIFT OF II BLUE SHIELD MENHIRS WITH EVERY **SLAVE** PURCHASED

PEOPLE DON'T EVEN WANT THEM AS A GIFT... WELL, THAT'S TOO BAD! I'VE LOST A FORTUNE, BUT LET'S FORGET IT...

THE THING IS...

YES?

WELL, IT'S LIKE THIS, O CAESAR...

I WANTED TO KEEP THE PEACE IN GAUL, SO BEFORE I LEFT I GAVE ORDERS FOR THEM TO GO ON BUYING MENHIRS... AND RAISING THE PRICE.

WHAT? YOU KNOW THE STATE OF MY FINANCES? AND YOU SAID WE'D MAKE A KILLING! GET BACK TO GAUL AND STOP IT!!!

ER...YOU WOULDN'T LIKE TO SEND SOMEONE ELSE, WOULD YOU? I HAVE A FRIEND WHO WAS AT BUSINESS SCHOOL WITH ME. HE...

YOU'RE GOING YOURSELF, YOU IDIOT! IT'S YOUR FAULT I NEARLY HAD A CIVIL WAR ON MY HANDS! ROME MIGHT HAVE BEEN RUINED! EVEN BRUTUS HAS BEEN GIVING ME NASTY LOOKS!

BUT...BUT THEY'LL KILL ME!

THAT PARTICULAR KILLING WOULDN'T WORRY ME!

ANYWAY, IF YOU DON'T GO I'LL HAVE YOU THROWN TO THE LIONS!!

MENHIR GRAVEYARD

BUT THE WORLD MENHIR CRISIS HAS NOT YET AFFECTED THE GAULISH VILLAGE...

ASTERIX! DOGMATIX!

?!

LISTEN... CAN I GO HUNTING BOARS WITH YOU?

WHAT, AN INFLUENTIAL MAN LIKE YOU? DON'T YOU HAVE A CONFERENCE? DON'T YOU HAVE A BUSINESS LUNCH?

PLEASE DON'T LAUGH AT ME. I KNOW I'VE BEEN SILLY. I'M BORED, AND I'VE HAD ENOUGH! EVERYONE HAS LOTS OF SESTERTII NOW! EVERYONE'S THE MOST INFLUENTIAL MAN IN THE VILLAGE!

I WANT TO BE FRIENDS AGAIN! I WANT TO HUNT BOAR! I WANT TO HAVE FUN...

BOOOHOOO!

WERE YOU THINKING OF HUNTING BOARS IN THAT GET-UP?

SNIFF... HMPH?

I'LL BE RIGHT BACK!

TEEHEE!

44

FULLIAUTOM TODAY

THAT ROMAN TOLD ME HE NEVER WANTED TO SEE ANOTHER MENHIR IN HIS LIFE!

HO!

BUT... BUT... WHAT'S TO BE BECOME OF ME? HOW AM I GOING TO PAY ALL THE PEOPLE WORKING FOR ME?

I'M GLAD TO HEAR IT! NOW I'LL BE ABLE TO GET MY SHIELD-BEARERS BACK!

LOOK!

OBELIX HAS STOPPED MAKING MENHIRS!

SO HE KNEW THE ROMANS WOULDN'T BE BUYING ANY MORE ... AND HE DIDN'T WARN US!

AND IT'S ALL HIS FAULT WE STARTED MAKING MENHIRS IN THE FIRST PLACE!

HE'S A TRAITOR!

IT'S ALL HIS DOING!

WE OUGHT TO TEACH HIM A LESSON!

HOLD THIS, WILL YOU, ASTERIX?

WITH PLEASURE.

COME ON, DOGMATIX!

GRRRRRRRRR

HOW NICE TO SEE THE VILLAGE RETURN TO ITS GOOD OLD WAYS!

YES, THERE'S NOTHING LIKE THE DAILY ROUND, THE COMMON TASK...

YOU DID VERY WELL. I'M PLEASED WITH YOU.

WAIT A MINUTE. LET'S TIE ALL THIS UP!

STOP, EVERYBODY! LISTEN TO ME!

SORRY TO DISTURB YOU, BUT WHY DON'T WE PAY A LITTLE CALL ON THE ROMANS INSTEAD OF FIGHTING EACH OTHER? AFTER ALL, THEY STARTED THE WHOLE THING!

YEAH!

HE'S RIGHT!

I WANT TO THANK YOU FOR YOUR LOVELY BIRTHDAY PRESENT, SO THIS TIME THE ROMANS ARE ON ME!

HOW ABOUT IT, O CHIEF VITALSTATISTIX?

LET'S GET THEM, BY TOUTATIS!

I STILL DON'T GET IT... JUST TELL ME HOW THE GAULS ARE GOING TO REACT NOW YOU'RE NOT BUYING ANY MORE OF THEIR MENHIRS...?

BECAUSE BEFORE YOU CAME ALONG, PLAYING THE FOOL, WE WERE WAITING QUIETLY FOR OUR RELIEF, WE WERE!

I'VE COMPLETED MY MISSION! LET ME GO!

WATCH OUT, MATES! HERE COME THE...

? ?

POC!

?!

THE GAU... THE GAU...

43A

43B

47

 proost Turnhout (Belgium)

PRINTED IN BELG